A NOTE ON THE TYPE

This book was set in Kiddish, a typeface designed by Gigantico; Always In My Heart, a typeface designed by By the Butterfly; and Amatic, a typeface designed by Vernon Adams.

First American edition published in 2013 by Enchanted Lion Books, 351 Van Brunt Street, Brooklyn, NY 11231
First published in France in 2001 by Mila Éditions as **Fantômes de Maisons**. Copyright © 2001 Mila Éditions.
English-language edition copyright © 2013 Enchanted Lion Books. Translated from the French by Claudia Z. Bedrick.
Jacket hand-lettered by Ohara Hale. Design and layout by Lawrence Kim.
ISBN: 978-1-59270-142-1. Printed and bound in August 2013 by South China Printing Company

For my two "J's":
One, a little ghost;
the other, not.   S.G.

Many little things in
this book are dedicated
to Oscar and Camille.
A big thank you to Anne.

M.B.

Boo...
I'm a ghost.

Umm...I don't think so.
That would really surprise me.

ME, I'm a ghost.

GHOSTS

WORDS by
Sonia GOLDIE

PICTURES by
Marc BOUTAVANT

What about me, then?

YOU, you're a torn old
sheet that's full of holes.

ENCHANTED LION BOOKS
NEW YORK

All right—it's time to tell the truth
about ghosts, because everything that's been
said about us is completely ridiculous.

For example, we don't live only in castles
or big old houses, and we certainly don't
drag around a ball and chain.

Except, perhaps, for a few
nostalgic ghosts who still cling
to the old stories.

Also, ghosts don't go
around saying,
"Boo...Boo... Boo..."
all day.

Who's that in the fireplace? Does he take himself for Santa Claus, or what? WELL NOW...It's Smokestack, who used to be WHITE as chalk with a silvery shimmer but is now completely covered in soot. Take a look: he's black as COAL. This is definitely a ghost to AVOID! If you don't, he'll billow into your living room like a tornado of black smoke. To get rid of him, make a fire and throw on plenty of logs. When he sees the smoke rising up through the chimney, he'll get restless and rise up with it. And this will be a good thing, because he's at his best when he's out in the fresh air, hovering in the sky. There, you might even mistake him for a cloud.

Oh, fudgecakes! Another spot!

A mysterious ghost is prowling through houses. As it's been reported, he will sit down right next to you as soon as you turn on your TV. He never smiles, just stares at the screen without moving. But if he sees things that scare him, he'll grab you, crying with fear, even though you won't be able to hear him. WATCH OUT, CHILDREN! Don't let him touch you. If he does, you'll get a chill in your back that runs straight through to your bones. Keep away from the screen. Turn off the TV. Just one more minute and it will be too late. The TV ghost will have arrived!

IT'S TOO LATE! He's already here!

You might think that this ghost never moves, but you'd be wrong!

He moves through paintings, giving beauty and energy to still lifes and landscapes.

Ah! A walk in the countryside: poppy red, ultramarine blue, grass green. For him, this is true happiness!

Follow him into the land of paintings. This ghost loves adventure and sees all of life in PICTURES ...

Signed:

THE PICTURE GHOST

Look closely. Do you see a little gray dot? Maybe...? If you squint a little? This ghost hides himself in portraits to see without being seen. You may be the one looking at the painting, but he's secretly gazing out at YOU, fixing an image of you in his mind!

Here, he's eating cheese!

If you manage to catch a glimpse of HIM, it will be because he often gets tripped up by color!

THE GHOST OF THE LIBRARY

Wherever there are books, he's there. Thin as a sheet of paper, he glides between the pages of his favorite books, where he stays for hours on end. He often falls asleep there, even if he's in the middle of a chapter. If you see the corner of a page turned down, you'll know he's been there! This is a very smart ghost, with the memory of an elephant.

But he's also very shy and doesn't dare show himself. He would rather live in his daydreams, wandering into the rooms of children who love books. Shh! Don't move...Perhaps he's right here, leaning on your shoulder so he can read what is being said about him!

SQUAFUMPF...The door of the refrigerator is pulled open. PLOP! A package falls to the floor. Who's that moving around in the kitchen?

It's a gluttonous ghost that devours anything and everything that's white. Sugar: YUM! Milk: SLURP!

White cheese, white rice, white glop...YUM! More yogurt goes down into the belly of this ghost than will ever go into yours. He gobbles, he gulps, and swallows.

SPLAAAATCH! He's spilled the milk! WHOOPS! Now there's flour everywhere! This is definitely a clumsy ghost, so you'd do best not to invite him to your house.

But if angel food cake and creamed rice happen to be your specialties, he still might come right in through your window and sit down at your table with you!

THE BATHROOM GHOST

How disgusting!

To begin with, this ghost has never washed. EVER! Not his hair, his nails, his teeth or his feet.

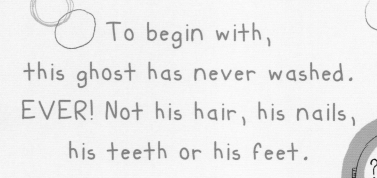

WHY?

Because he hates water. Sadly, a terrible curse has forced him to spend his entire life in the bathroom.

THAT'S SO SAD!

He'd like to run away like water but can't, so whenever you get out of the bathtub, all clean and sweet-smelling, he gets really sad. If he could cry, he would wake up the whole neighborhood! When the whole family washes up, he tries to escape through a drain or faucet, but he's too big to get away that way. So he hides behind a bathrobe or under a pile of towels, where he takes comfort in his own salty smell.

the GHOST of the NIGHT

This ghost is a cunning one! So look under your bed before going to sleep, because if you don't scare him away first, he'll be there, waiting for night to come!

Once it's dark, he awakes. Moving about on cat's feet, he likes to make a big mess by tossing clothes and turning on the toys.

Who tickles your feet? Who pulls the sleeve of your pajamas? Who yanks down the curtains and makes those little snorts?

It's him!

He smirks as he watches you. If you sleep very soundly, he'll slide into your dreams—or, even worse, into your

NIGHTMARES!

But in the morning...
Poof!
There's no one there.

He's a clever one!

Hey there, I saw you!
Put that book down immediately!
Don't touch that!
I'm going to get all red and angry if I see any of you move!
Go play in your own room!
Jumping on the bed is completely out of the question!
Don't open that drawer!
I live in your parents' bedroom and I forbid you to come in!
DO NOT ENTER!
Is that clear? Get out of here, all of you! I don't ever want to see you again.
You have your toys, your teddy bears and your puppets!
Go play by yourselves for a little while. I mean
REALLY!

This old, gentle ghost, who is wrinkly yet twinkly, likes to spend his time remembering the good old days.

He also likes to dress up—as a marquis, a pirate, even an Arabian prince, so he delves into trunks of old clothes and slips into shoes that are too big and too small.

the ghost of the attic

Spread out on the floor, with his nose in the dust, he reads old newspapers, listens to old, scratched records, entertains himself with broken cassettes, and wraps himself in silvery scarves to scare away the spiders.

If you catch sight of this ghost, he'll be sure to tell you all about his adventures, as well as stories from long ago and from long before that, too.

Perhaps, even, from the time of your great grandfather, which was before this old ghost had even been born...

This delicate ghost is almost transparent. He can barely be seen: a small movement of the curtain, a slight breeze. That's all you'll see. He only likes winter, when it is cold outside and warm inside, because only then is he able to draw pictures in the steam on the window panes. He watches the snowflakes fall and remembers playing in the snow when he was little. The big snowman reminds him a little of his cousin! When spring returns and the windows are opened, the ghost from behind the curtain heads for colder climates. But don't worry, he'll return next winter for sure!

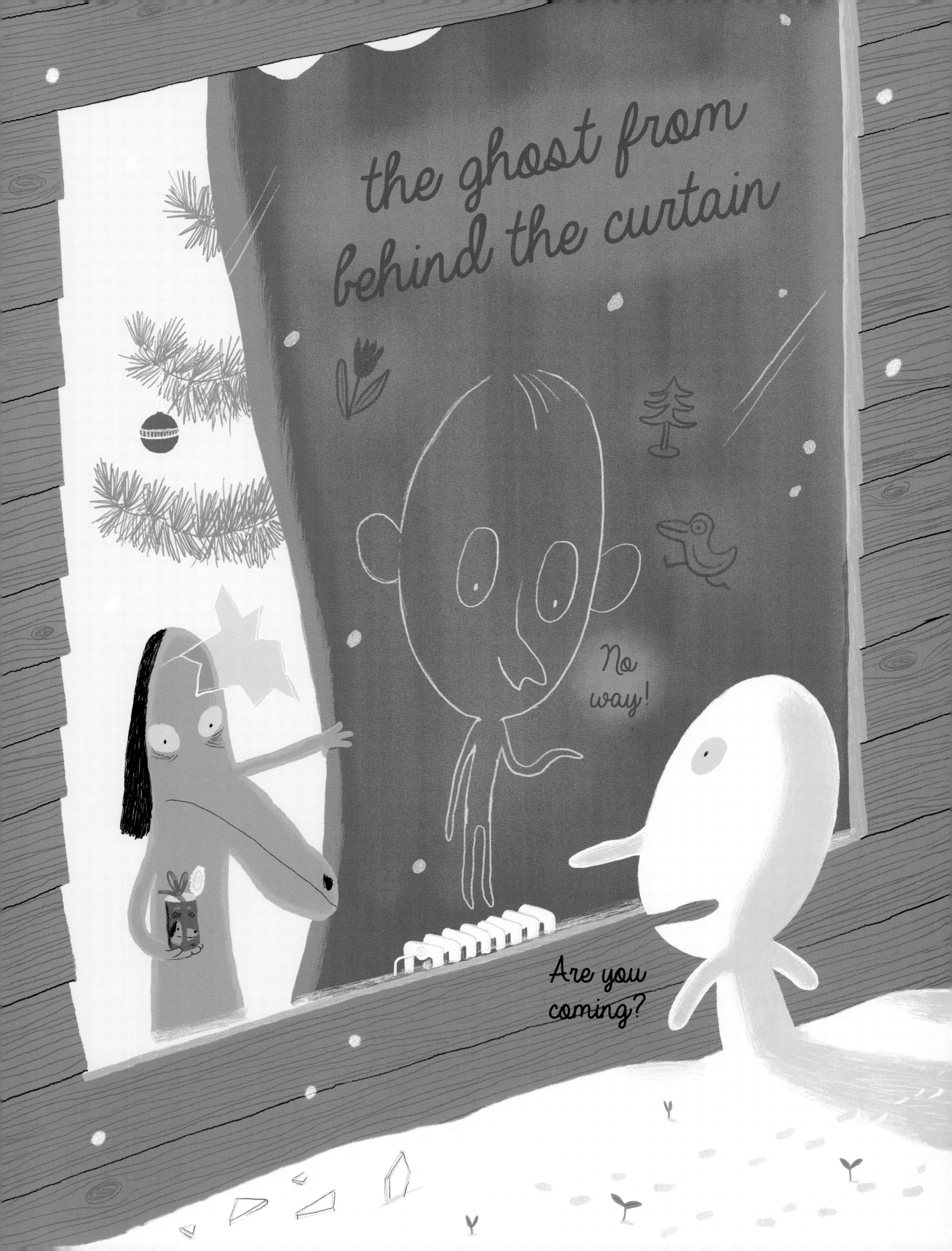
the ghost from behind the curtain
No way!
Are you coming?

THE GARDEN GHOST

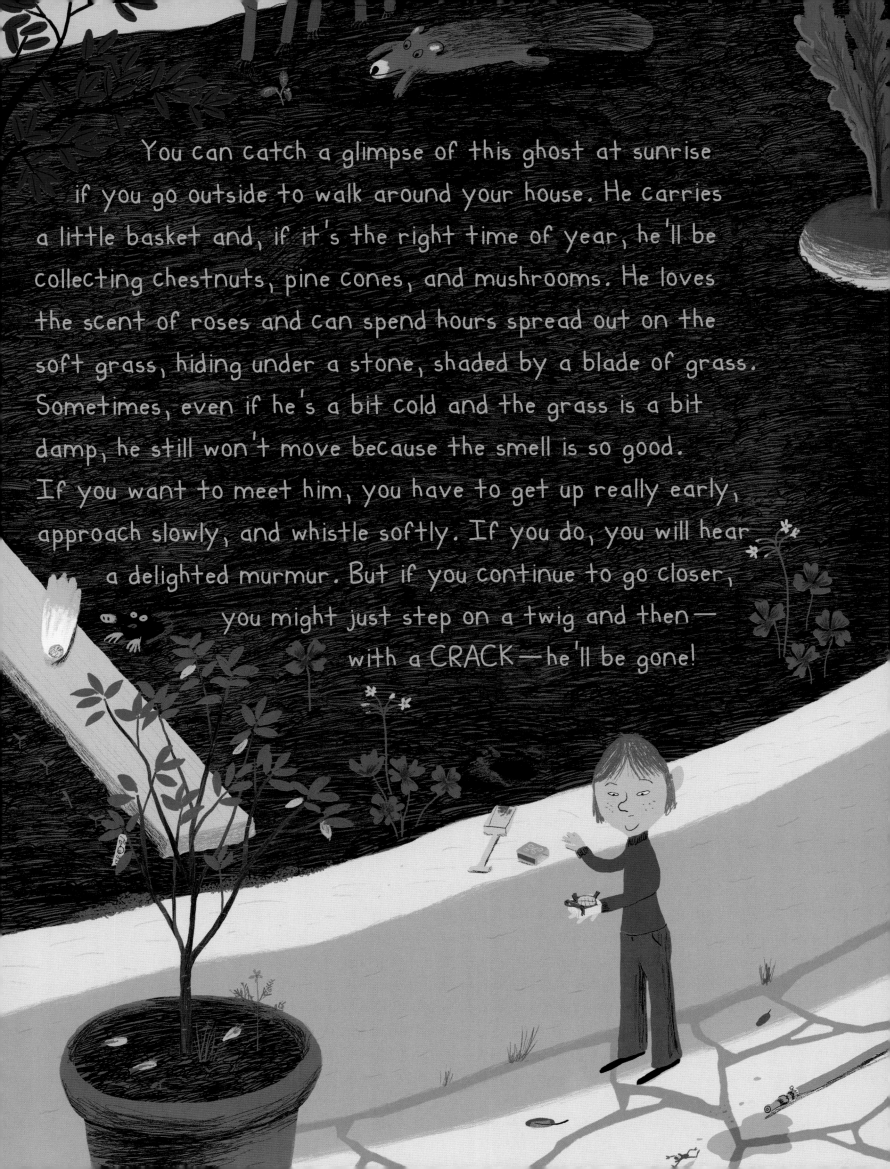

You can catch a glimpse of this ghost at sunrise
if you go outside to walk around your house. He carries
a little basket and, if it's the right time of year, he'll be
collecting chestnuts, pine cones, and mushrooms. He loves
the scent of roses and can spend hours spread out on the
soft grass, hiding under a stone, shaded by a blade of grass.
Sometimes, even if he's a bit cold and the grass is a bit
damp, he still won't move because the smell is so good.
If you want to meet him, you have to get up really early,
approach slowly, and whistle softly. If you do, you will hear
a delighted murmur. But if you continue to go closer,
you might just step on a twig and then—
with a CRACK—he'll be gone!

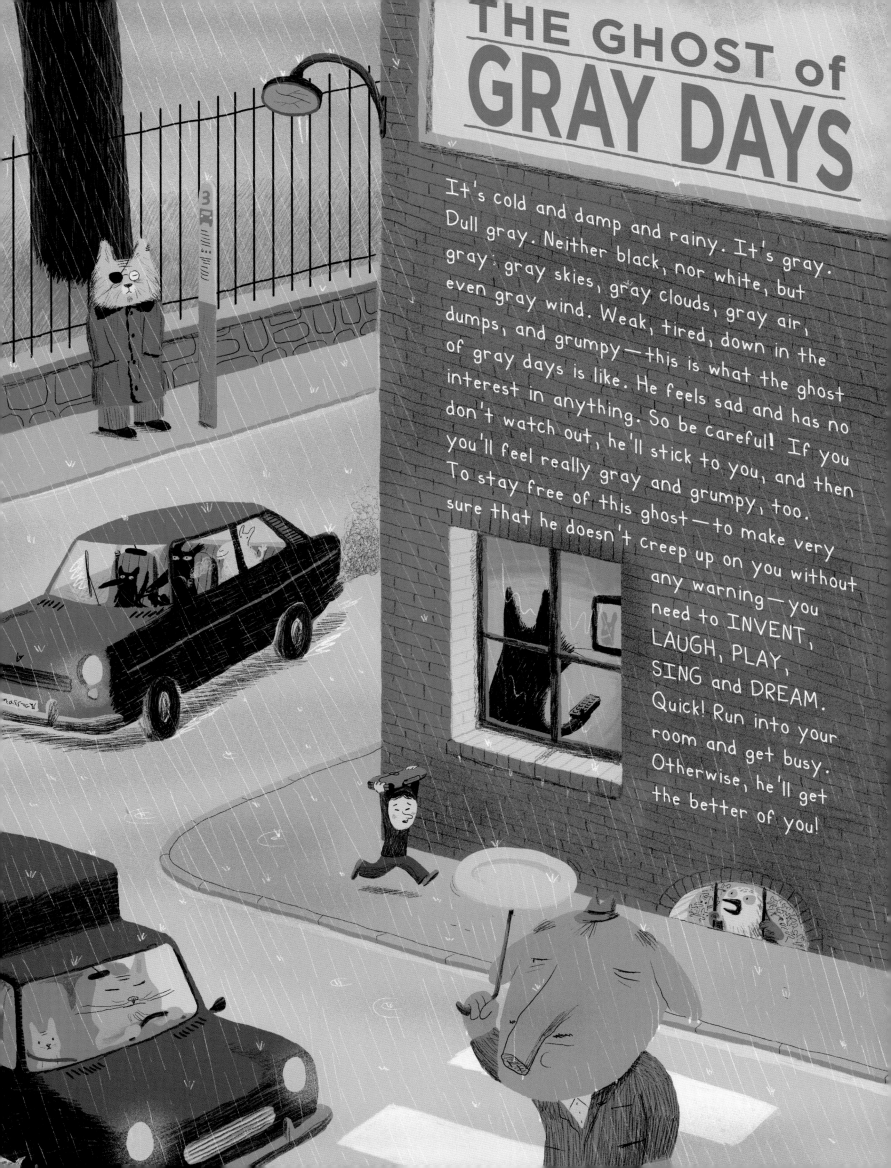

THE GHOST of GRAY DAYS

It's cold and damp and rainy. It's gray. Dull gray. Neither black, nor white, but gray; gray skies, gray clouds, gray air, even gray wind. Weak, tired, down in the dumps, and grumpy—this is what the ghost of gray days is like. He feels sad and has no interest in anything. So be careful! If you don't watch out, he'll stick to you, and then you'll feel really gray and grumpy, too. To stay free of this ghost—to make very sure that he doesn't creep up on you without any warning—you need to INVENT, LAUGH, PLAY, SING and DREAM. Quick! Run into your room and get busy. Otherwise, he'll get the better of you!

the GHOST
of the
BASEMENT

Hmm...This is definitely not a sweet-smelling ghost. He suffers from rheumatism, blows his nose with spider webs and fills bottles with snot. His odor of rotten potatoes and old mushrooms is really gross to the other ghosts, so he wasn't invited to tonight's party. Poor ghost!

the
GHOST
of the
WASHING
MACHINE

Spinning around in the machine day after day has turned this ghost into a little ball. In the machine's tub, which is his home, you will find his bed of hair, along with all the little balls of paper that he's chewed. And if you're really lucky, you just might find his treasures, too!

the GHOST of the TELEPHONE

Dring! A ring, and then nothing. Someone's hung up on you. Or maybe you hear voices and a conversation in the background? That's him, too! You see, this ghost sleeps in the receiver, with his feet in the microphone, which is why your phone doesn't always smell quite right.

the GHOST of the GARAGE

A squeaky jack? Hurrah! It's time to get some grub! This ghost's favorite meal is the car oil drippings that taste like french fries, but he doesn't eat only that! Toast with dirty lubricating oil from the breaks, gasoline tea with hot rubber cake! And for dessert, a little dish of exhaust! Ah...there's nothing better!

Come join us
at the
ghost ball!